Merry merry Christmas
to Owen + Bix
Winifred and.
of course,  (Max)

For Carleton and, of course, for Max

Max Moves to Moscow copyright © Frances Lincoln Limited 2006
Text and illustrations copyright © Winifred Riser 2006

First published in Great Britain in 2006
and in the USA in 2007 by Frances Lincoln Children's Books, 4 Torriano Mews,
Torriano Avenue, London NW5 2RZ

Distributed in the USA by Publishers Group West

www.franceslincoln.com

British Library Cataloguing in Publication Data
available on request

ISBN 10:1-84507-482-3
ISBN 13: 978-1-84507-482-1

The illustrations are done in watercolour.

Printed in China
1 3 5 7 9 8 6 4 2

Max Moves to
MOSCOW

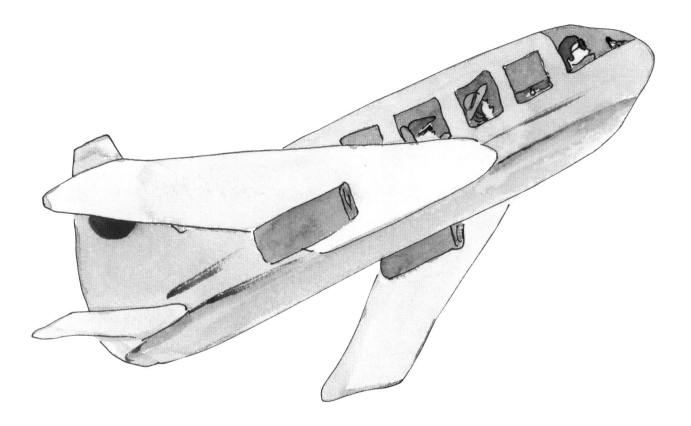

Winifred Riser

F

FRANCES LINCOLN
CHILDREN'S BOOKS

Max was a happy dog. It didn't take much for Max to have a good day, just a shining sun and a bouncing ball.

Every day Max ate his breakfast and played in the garden. But on this particular morning there was so much banging and clanging inside the house that Max could not concentrate.

Max went to investigate the noise, and to his surprise,
the house was empty except for stacks and stacks
of big brown boxes and bulging suitcases.

Max knew that all the boxes could only mean
one thing – a trip. And Max was crazy about trips!

Soon everything was packed, even Max!
He said goodbye to his friends from
the window of a very full car.
Max was excited and nervous.
He had never been packed
before. This seemed like
a very big trip.

Max was very excited when he saw
the aeroplane.
   The journey was so long that
he fell fast asleep. He slept and slept
as the plane flew through the night.

When Max woke up, he was in a place called Moscow.
As Max looked around, he was pretty sure he wanted
to go back home. Everything was very cold and very white.

That night, Max looked out at his new home.
It didn't look like anything he had ever seen.
It was all very strange. Were there other dogs
in Moscow?

In the morning Max went to the park.
He had never seen snow before and he could
not decide if it was soft or prickly, but it was
definitely cold. Max began to sniff around
to learn more about it.

He heard a familiar sound coming from
behind a tree.

'There are other dogs in Moscow!' thought Max,
wagging his tail. 'Perhaps they can tell me about
snow. Perhaps they will play with me, too.'

The first dog Max met was Sasha.
Sasha showed Max her newest trick.
She had learned to say *Preevet!*

"That means 'hello' in Russian,"
she explained.

So Max said, "*Preevet, Sasha!*"

Then Max met Boris. Max said "*Preevet,*" but Boris
only replied, "Harrumph!"

Boris didn't like making new friends, but Max thought
he saw Boris's tail wag just a bit.

Max bounded over to Bronnya.
She was very shy and many things
frightened her, especially strange dogs.
So Bronnya hid behind a tree.

From there, she whispered,
"Preevet, Max."

Then Max said hello to old Uncle Vanya.
"Preevet," said Max.

"Welcome to the neighbourhood, Max,"
said Uncle Vanya, and he fell asleep right
there in the snow.

Next morning Max woke up early,
grabbed his ball and ran to the park.
All his new friends were there!
   "*Preevet!*" he said,
and threw his ball into the air.

Sasha had never seen a dog throw a ball
so she came over to play. Max and Sasha were
having such fun that Bronnya bounded over.
Then gruff Boris barked and joined in the
game too. It was so exciting that he forgot
to be grumpy.

The dogs woke up Uncle Vanya.
But Uncle Vanya yawned and mumbled,
"You know what they say about old dogs…"
And he fell right back to sleep.

Just then a strange thing happened.
The ball disappeared. The dogs looked
and looked and sniffed and sniffed,
but no one could find it.

    They even looked under lazy Uncle Vanya
but they couldn't find it anywhere!

The next day, Max brought another ball.
They played and played and even Uncle Vanya
joined in.

But, once again, the ball disappeared.
They just couldn't find it anywhere.

It was late and the dogs were getting tired.
They said, "*Paka,*" which means 'goodbye'
in Russian, and went home.

Every day, Max brought a new ball…
…and every day the new ball
disappeared.

At last Max ran out of balls and the dogs couldn't play any more. Had someone stolen the balls? It wasn't Sasha because she liked the game too much. Boris had nowhere to hide them.

It couldn't be Bronnya, because she was too good at the game to want to stop, and Uncle Vanya was too lazy to take them. It was very mysterious.

Without the balls, the park was not much fun.
Boris became grumpy again and Bronnya just
sat quietly. Sasha wasn't interested in learning
any new tricks and Uncle Vanya, of course, fell asleep.

One night the snow stopped falling and it started
to rain in Moscow. It rained and rained and rained
and no one went to the park.

When the sun finally came out,
Max couldn't wait to see his friends.
They shouted happily, "Preevet, Max!
Come quickly! Look what we've found!"

There, floating in the puddles,
were the missing balls!

"They must have been buried
in the snow," said Bronnya happily.
"The snow had hidden them all!"

Sasha rolled over with excitement
and Boris forgot to be a grump.

All summer long there were lots of balls for the dogs
to play with. Max loved his new home in Moscow.
Now every day was a good one for Max
and his friends.

About Moscow

St Basil's Cathedral
Russia's most famous church,
St. Basil's was built by Ivan the Terrible
and named after Moscow's Holy Fool,
Basil (Vasily). It is in Red Square.

Patriarch's Pond
This is Max's favourite park in Moscow.
Russian children have ice-skated here
for 300 years and dogs have played
in the snow for just as long.

Christ the Saviour Cathedral
This church was built in the 1880s
and was torn down, turned into
a swimming pool, and then rebuilt again.
It is the biggest church in Russia.

**State Historical Museum
and Red Square**
In Russian the word for 'red' originally
meant 'beautiful' and Red Square
is beautiful. This famous public square
is at the very centre of Moscow.

Moscow State University
This is Russia's oldest university.
The tall building has the best views
of the whole city, and legend has it
that there are many secret
tunnels underneath it.

Kremlin Wall
The whole city of Moscow
used to fit behind these high walls,
built to keep the city safe from attacking
armies. Today, the Russian government
is based in the Kremlin.

Kuskovo Estate

This palace is so big
it has three separate parks, a pond,
pools, and a church. A long time ago,
it even had its own private zoo!

Novodevichy Convent

Many Russian tsars (kings) sent
their wives and daughters to live
their whole lives in this beautiful
500-year-old convent.

About Max

I am a three-year-old black Labrador.
I live with my mum and dad in Moscow, Russia. I enjoy going
on adventures, having my belly rubbed and playing
catch in the park. This is the first book starring me. I hope
there will be more. I get treats when
I pose for pictures!